PANO the Train

by Sharon Holaves

illustrated by Gia...

GOLDEN PRESS
Western Publishing Company, Inc.
Racine, Wisconsin

Third Printing, 1978

TOOT-TOOT

DING-DING

CHUG-CHUGGED

These simple pictures are signals for you and your child. They will appear throughout this story. After your child knows the signals, he will be able to "read" the book with you. Just point to each as you come to it, and let him provide the sound he has learned. Happy chugging!

Every morning, Pano stoked himself with coal
and filled his boiler with water. Every morning,
Pano counted the cars that he pulled, from the
coal car to the red caboose.

Then, every morning,
he blew his whistle ▐▐▐ (toot-toot),
rang his bell 🔔🔔🔔 (ding-ding),

and slowly  (chug-chugged)
out of the mountain village.

One morning, as Pano  past the village
meadow, something very strange happened. The

goats and sheep in the village meadow didn't baa "Good morning." Instead, all the goats and sheep turned their heads to look at Pano, and in very loud voices, they baaed, "You've lost . . . you've lost. . . ."

Pano blew his whistle 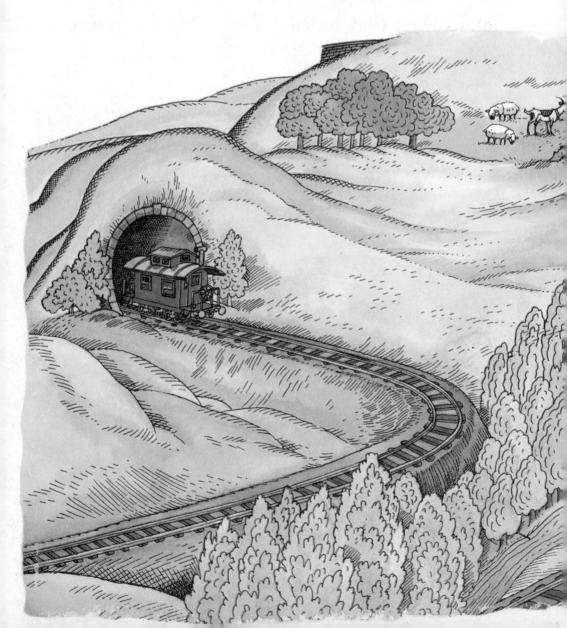 at their baaing.
He thought, "I've lost what? A race?"

He didn't want to lose a race that morning,
so he ☁☁☁ even harder.

Pano blew his whistle  at all the chickens and ducks in their yard. The chickens and ducks jumped and fluttered. They loudly clucked and quacked at Pano: "You've lost ... you've lost. ..."

He rang his bell 🔔🔔🔔 at the silly chickens and ducks, and he ☁☁☁ even faster.

Down the mountain Pano rolled.

Near the tracks, some pigs snoozed in the warm mud. Pano rang his bell 🔔🔔🔔 at the snoozing, muddy pigs.

His bell woke the pigs.
The pigs raised their snouts
from the warm mud and grunted at him:
"You've lost . . . you've lost. . . ."

Pano didn't ring his bell. He didn't even
blow his whistle. He just
as hard and as fast as he could.

In the valley, puffing and panting,
Pano  along near the sea.

The fishermen were throwing their nets into the water. Pano rang his bell 🔔🔔🔔 and blew his whistle ▮▮▮ at the fishermen. But the fishermen only shook their nets into the water and called, "You've lost . . . you've lost. . . ."

Finally the weary engine  around the long bend to the village in the valley. He thought puzzled, unhappy thoughts. "The sheep and the goats, the chickens and the ducks, the pigs, and all the fishermen say I lost. Who was racing with me?"

Pano looked far down the tracks, trying to see the winner of the race. There was only a red caboose in front of the station.

And then, as he came closer to the station, he saw what the sheep and goats in the meadow had seen. He saw what the clucking, quacking chickens and ducks had seen. He saw what the snoozing pigs in the warm mud had seen. He saw what the fishermen with their nets had seen.

He hadn't been in a race at all. What he had lost was his own beautiful red caboose!

The goats and the sheep, the chickens and the ducks, the pigs, and the fishermen had been saying, "You've lost... you've lost your red caboose."

Pano gave a long, tired whistle ⸮⸮⸮⸮⸮⸮ . He slowly 🌫🌫🌫 to the station in the valley. And there, in front of the station, sat Pano's beautiful red caboose! It had rolled down the other side of the mountain.

Pano hadn't lost either a race *or* a caboose, but Pano had learned to listen.